THE BOOKS ABOUT JOSEFINA

❋

Also available in Spanish

JOSEFINA
SAVES
THE DAY

A SUMMER STORY

BY VALERIE TRIPP

ILLUSTRATIONS JEAN-PAUL TIBBLES

VIGNETTES SUSAN McALILEY

PLEASANT COMPANY

Published by Pleasant Company Publications
© Copyright 1998 by Pleasant Company
All rights reserved. No part of this book may be used or reproduced
in any manner whatsoever without written permission except in the
case of brief quotations embodied in critical articles and reviews.
For information, address: Book Editor, Pleasant Company Publications,
8400 Fairway Place, P.O. Box 620998, Middleton, WI 53562.

Printed in the United States of America.
98 99 00 01 02 03 WCT 10 9 8 7 6 5 4 3 2 1

The American Girls Collection®, Josefina®, and Josefina Montoya™
are trademarks of Pleasant Company.

PERMISSIONS & PICTURE CREDITS
The following individuals and organizations have generously given permission to reprint
illustrations contained in "Looking Back": pp. 62-63—Jack Parsons Photography, Santa Fe, NM
(landscapes); photo by Philip E. Harroun, courtesy of the Museum of New Mexico, Santa Fe,
neg. #11326 (procession); pp. 64-65—*Tiaguis* by Casimiro Castro, courtesy of the Colección Banco
de México, Mexico City. Photographed by Arturo Chapa (plaza); sketch by Theodore R. Davis,
courtesy of the Museum of New Mexico, Santa Fe, neg. #31339 (Santa Fe street); History
Collections, Los Angeles County Museum of Natural History (shoes); Franz Meyer Museum,
Mexico City (jar); School of American Research Collections, Museum of New Mexico, Santa Fe,
photographed by Douglas Kahn (Pueblo pot); courtesy of The Toledo Museum of Art,
Toledo, OH. Gift of Edward Drummond Libbey, #1917.373 (flask); image reproduced from
Eyewitness: Costume with permission from DK Publishing, Inc., New York, NY (bonnet);
sketch by Frederick Remington (trapper); pp. 66-67—courtesy of the Richard F. Brush
Art Gallery, St. Lawrence University, Canton, NY (wagon train); courtesy of the
Museum of New Mexico, Santa Fe, neg. #144638 (fandango).

Edited by Peg Ross and Judith Woodburn
Designed by Mark Macauley, Myland McRevey, Laura Moberly, and Jane S. Varda
Art Directed by Jane S. Varda

Library of Congress Cataloging-in-Publication Data

Tripp, Valerie, 1951-
Josefina saves the day : a summer story / by Valerie Tripp ;
illustrations [by] Jean-Paul Tibbles ; vignettes [by] Susan McAliley. — 1st ed.

p. cm. — (The American girls collection)
"Book five"—P. [1] of cover.
Summary: In 1825 when Josefina trusts a trader in Santa Fe with an important deal, she makes
a surprising discovery about this young American who leaves town without paying her.
ISBN 1-56247-590-8 (hardcover). — ISBN 1-56247-589-4 (pbk.)
[1. Trust (Psychology)—Fiction. 2. Mexican Americans—Fiction.
3. New Mexico—History—To 1848—Fiction.]
I. Tibbles, Jean-Paul, ill. II. Title. III. Series.
PZ7.T7363Jp 1998 [Fic]—DC21 98-4959 CIP AC

TO KATHY BORKOWSKI,
VAL HODGSON, PEG ROSS,
JANE VARDA, AND JUDY WOODBURN
WITH THANKS

Josefina and her family speak
Spanish, so you'll see some
Spanish words in this book.
If you can't tell what a word
means from reading the story
or looking at the illustrations,
you can turn to the "Glossary
of Spanish Words" that begins
on page 68. It will tell you what
the word means and how to
pronounce it.

Remember that in Spanish,
"j" is pronounced like "h."
That means Josefina's name is
pronounced "ho-seh-FEE-nah."

TABLE OF CONTENTS

JOSEFINA'S FAMILY
AND FRIENDS

PAPÁ
*Josefina's father, who
guides his family
and his rancho with
quiet strength.*

ANA
*Josefina's oldest sister,
who is married and has
two little boys.*

JOSEFINA
*A ten-year-old girl
whose heart and hopes
are as big as the
New Mexico sky.*

FRANCISCA
*Josefina's sixteen-year-old
sister, who is headstrong
and impatient.*

CLARA
*Josefina's practical,
sensible sister, who is
thirteen years old.*

TÍA DOLORES
*Josefina's aunt, who
lives with Josefina's
family on their rancho.*

PATRICK O'TOOLE
*A scout for an American
wagon train traveling
on the Santa Fe Trail.*

ABUELITO
*Josefina's grandfather,
a trader who lives in
Santa Fe.*

ABUELITA
*Josefina's gracious,
dignified grandmother,
who values tradition.*

THE BIRD-SHAPED FLUTE

High up on a breezy hilltop, Josefina Montoya sat playing her clay flute.

The flute was shaped like a bird and sounded like one, too. When Josefina played it, a clear, fine tune just like a bird's whistle looped through the air into the blue, blue sky.

It was July. Josefina and her family were visiting her grandfather's *rancho*, which was about a mile from the center of Santa Fe. Josefina loved this hilltop behind Abuelito's house. From here she could see the flat rooftops of buildings in Santa Fe and the narrow streets that zigzagged between them. She could see the slender silvery ribbon that was the Santa Fe River, and the long road that led home

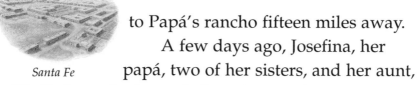

Santa Fe

to Papá's rancho fifteen miles away.

A few days ago, Josefina, her papá, two of her sisters, and her aunt, Tía Dolores, had traveled on that road to come to Abuelito's rancho. The trip was hot and dusty, but Josefina had been too excited to mind. She and her family had worked, planned, and looked forward to the trip for almost a year.

They were traveling for a very important reason. They needed to be in Santa Fe when the wagon train from the United States arrived. Papá had brought mules and blankets with him to trade with the *americanos*. Josefina had woven some of the blankets herself, which made her pleased and proud. She understood how much depended on this trade. If the americanos paid well for the mules and the blankets, Papá would be able to replace his sheep that had been killed in a terrible flood last fall. If Papá could not replace the sheep, it would be a hard, hungry winter for everyone on the rancho. They needed sheep for food and for wool to weave. Josefina had prayed and prayed that Papá's trading with the americanos would go well.

Josefina and her sisters couldn't wait to see the

fine and fancy things the americanos would bring. There'd be toys and shoes and material for dresses that had come hundreds of miles on the Santa Fe Trail, all the way from the United States! The wagon train was expected to arrive any day now, and Josefina was keeping a lookout for it. As soon as she'd finished her chores this morning, she'd climbed up here to her favorite hilltop to look at the southeast horizon. She was hoping to see a cloud of dust stirred up by the wagon train, but the horizon looked the same as always.

Just now, though, Josefina *heard* something new. It sounded as if a real bird were singing along with her clay flute. Josefina stopped playing and tilted her head to listen. Then she grinned. It wasn't a real bird at all. It was a person whistling.

"*Buenos días!*" Josefina called out. She turned, expecting to see that the whistler was one of her sisters who'd come to watch for the wagon train, too. But it wasn't. The whistler was a young man Josefina had never seen before. Josefina scrambled to her feet so quickly she almost dropped her flute. The young man was a stranger. And not just any stranger, either. Josefina immediately folded her hands, bowed her head, and looked down at the ground, which was the polite way for a child to stand before an adult. But she could tell just by looking at the tips of the stranger's boots that they came from the United States. She knew because Abuelito had a pair of boots like them that he'd bought last summer from the americanos.

"Buenos días," said the young man. He spoke in Spanish, but with an accent Josefina had never heard before.

Josefina had a sudden, excited thought. The young man must be an americano who'd come ahead of the wagon train! Josefina was usually shy around strangers, but right now her curiosity was stronger than her shyness. If the young man was an americano, he'd be the first she'd ever met face to face. She raised her eyes and sneaked a peek. He had a very *nice* face, Josefina decided. He had blue eyes, a sunburned nose, and a friendly smile.

"Forgive me for surprising you," the stranger went on. "I thought you were a bird."

I thought you were a bird, too! Josefina almost said. She wanted to ask, *Please, señor, who* are *you?* But of

4

course she didn't. It wasn't good manners for a
child to ask a grownup questions. In fact, Josefina
wasn't sure whether it was proper for her to talk to
the stranger at all. Perhaps she should *act* like a bird
and fly away! But that didn't seem very polite.

While Josefina stood wondering what she should
do, the young man did something astonishing. He
took a case off his back, opened it, took out a violin,
and began to play. Josefina smiled when she realized
that he was playing the same notes that she had
played on her bird-shaped flute. The young man
wound the notes together into a tune that danced
in the air. When he finished, he swept his hat off
his head and bowed. "I'm Patrick O'Toole, from
Missouri," he said. "What is your name?"

"By God's grace," Josefina answered, "I am
Josefina Montoya."

"Josefina Montoya," Patrick repeated slowly.
"I'm glad to meet you. I'm looking for the home
of Señor Felipe Romero. Do you know him?"

"*Sí*," answered Josefina politely. "He's my
grandfather." She pointed to Abuelito's house
nearby. "He lives right here."

"Well, then, Señorita Josefina," said Patrick

"I'm Patrick O'Toole, from Missouri," he said. "What is your name?"

as he put his violin away. "Will you lead me to your grandfather's house?"

"I will," answered Josefina. "Please, follow me." She slipped the string of her clay flute around her neck and led Patrick down the hill. She couldn't help smiling a secret smile when she thought how surprised her family would be!

Abuelito's house was built around a center courtyard. The doors to the kitchen, the sleeping rooms, the weaving room, and the family *sala* opened onto it. Josefina led Patrick across the courtyard. She stopped outside the family sala, where her family was gathering for the mid-day meal. Abuelito had come to the door and was staring out at her.

"Abuelito," Josefina said respectfully. "Please permit me to introduce Señor Patrick O'Toole, from" —Josefina pronounced the English word carefully— "Missouri."

Abuelito was used to having unexpected guests, but this was the first time one of his granddaughters had brought a complete stranger to visit. And the stranger was an americano, too! But Abuelito was always a gracious host. *"Bienvenido,"* he said to Patrick. "You are welcome in my house, young man. Please come in."

"Thank you, sir," said Patrick. Josefina tapped her head to warn him to duck down so that he'd fit under the low doorway, and they both stepped inside. "I know you were expecting my father, who did business with you last summer, but—"

"Oh!" said Abuelito, as he realized who Patrick was. "You're the son of my friend, Señor O'Toole." Abuelito shook Patrick's hand. "Your father is a fine man. I hope he's in good health?"

"I believe so," said Patrick. "You see, he's farther south in Mexico, so he asked me to conduct his business here in—"

"Fine, fine," interrupted Abuelito. "There will be time for us to talk about business later, plenty of time."

Josefina could see that Patrick didn't understand. Abuelito would consider it very poor manners to discuss business matters right away, especially with someone he did not know. It was the custom in New Mexico to have a friendly conversation first, *then* talk about business.

Patrick tried again. "Well, sir," he began. No one saw Josefina tug on his sleeve. When Patrick glanced at her, she frowned and shook her head just the smallest bit to tell him no. Patrick looked confused for a moment, but then he seemed to understand. "As you say, sir," he said to Abuelito. "We can talk about business later."

"Good!" said Abuelito. "Allow me to introduce you to my family." He introduced Patrick to Papá, and then to Abuelita, Josefina's grandmother, and then to Tía Dolores.

"We're so glad Dolores is home for a visit," Abuelito said. "She's been away, staying on my son-in-law's rancho for almost a year now, helping him take care of his daughters since his own dear wife died. You've already met his youngest daughter, Josefina. His eldest, Ana, stayed home to help her husband look after the rancho. These are his daughters Francisca and Clara."

The sisters stood with their heads bowed. But Josefina saw Francisca studying Patrick from under her long, dark eyelashes.

"Please sit and have something to eat, señor," said Abuelita generously. "Honor us by joining us."

"*Gracias*," said Patrick.

Josefina sat between her sisters Francisca and Clara. Both sisters poked her and looked at her with raised eyebrows that said silently in sister language, *Oh, we can't wait to find out how you met the americano!* Josefina grinned back, pleased to have made her sisters curious.

During the meal, Abuelito kept the conversation away from business. He spoke to Patrick about the beautiful summer weather they were having and asked Patrick about weather in Missouri. Abuelita said nothing, but her sharp eyes never left Patrick's face. Papá didn't say anything either. But Josefina could tell that he was listening carefully to everything Patrick said.

I hope Papá likes Señor Patrick, Josefina thought. *I hope everyone does.* She was glad when Tía Dolores said to Patrick, "You speak Spanish well. How did you learn?"

"My father taught me," said Patrick. "I can't read or write Spanish at all, and I'm afraid I don't always remember the right words to say."

"You are doing fine," said Abuelito kindly.

In fact, Josefina thought Patrick was doing

beautifully. He stumbled over his words only once, and that was when Francisca poured him some tea. Patrick looked up at her and seemed to forget how to say thank you—or anything else. But Josefina had seen *that* happen to men who spoke perfect Spanish. Francisca was very beautiful.

Finally everyone had finished eating and the servants had cleared the table. Abuelito turned to Patrick. "Now," he said. "Tell us. When will the wagon train arrive?"

"Tomorrow morning, sir," said Patrick.

"That's good news!" said Abuelito. "But how is

11

it that you are here before the rest of the wagon train?"

"I'm one of the scouts," explained Patrick. "Scouts ride ahead of the wagon train. We find the safest places to cross rivers, the easiest passes through the mountains, and the best places to set up camp along the way."

"I'm sure you've had lots of adventures," said Abuelito.

"Not as many as you have, sir," said Patrick. "My father told me that you've been a trader on the *Camino Real* for many years. He said you've had adventures enough for twenty men!"

Abuelito was pleased. "I'll tell you about my adventures on the Camino Real sometime," he said.

"I'd like that," said Patrick. "You see, I'll be here in Santa Fe for about a week. I have to be ready to leave at a moment's notice. As soon as the captain of the wagon train gives me the word, I'll be heading down the Camino Real. Many of the americano traders are continuing farther south into Mexico when they leave Santa Fe, so the scouts have to go ahead of them and explore the route. Anything you can tell me would be a great help, Señor Romero."

"It will be a pleasure," said Abuelito.

"Thank you, sir," said Patrick. "Maybe you can help me in another way, too. The traders are going to need fresh mules for their trip down the Camino Real. They asked me to find some. Do you know anyone who has mules to sell or trade?"

Abuelito didn't answer right away. He glanced at Papá.

Josefina knew that Abuelito and Papá were being careful. Before they decided to do business with Patrick, they'd want to be sure he was honest and trustworthy. Papá had been watching Patrick as if he were trying to decide what sort of person the young man was.

Now Papá spoke slowly. "I have mules to trade," he said.

"Oh!" said Patrick. "May I see them, Señor Montoya?"

Papá nodded. "You may see them," he said. "Come with me." He stood and gestured toward the door.

Abuelito went outside and Patrick started to follow. But before he left, Patrick thanked Abuelita for her hospitality. Then he turned and smiled at Josefina. "I certainly am glad I heard that bird whistling on the hilltop," he said. "I hope I'll hear it again soon!"

Josefina smiled back.

After the men had left, Josefina and her sisters helped Abuelita and Tía Dolores tidy the room.

"So!" said Francisca to Josefina. "Where did you find the americano?"

"Well, I guess he found me," said Josefina. "I was on the hilltop looking for the wagon train and he surprised me."

"And *you* surprised *me*, Josefina," said Tía Dolores. She put her hands on her hips and smiled at Josefina. "I've always believed that you were shy of strangers. Not anymore, I see!"

"You and the americano seem to have become acquainted very quickly," said Clara.

"Too quickly," said Abuelita, frowning. "We don't really know this americano at all. How do we know he is truly Señor O'Toole's son? How do we know he is honest?" She shook her head. "All we know for certain is that he's very young. I hope your papá will be careful. I don't think it's wise to trust a stranger, especially when the business is so important!"

"Nothing is decided yet," said Tía Dolores quietly.

Abuelita went on. "If this young man isn't reliable, it'll be a terrible mistake to do business with him," she said.

Abuelita sighed and Josefina's shoulders drooped. She had been so proud to be the one who brought Patrick to her family! Would Papá be wrong to trust Patrick? Was *she* wrong to like Patrick?

Tía Dolores moved closer to Josefina. "How *did* you get acquainted with Señor Patrick so quickly?" she asked.

Josefina held up the little bird-shaped flute. "I was playing this clay flute that you gave me," she said. "Then Señor Patrick played the same song on his violin." She smiled, remembering. "The music sounded so friendly."

Tía Dolores laughed. "Music *can* sound friendly," she said. "Sometimes music can say things better than words can. Don't you think so, Josefina?"

"Sí!" said Josefina, cheered by Tía Dolores's understanding. She hurried to finish helping so that she could go outside. She wanted to play Patrick's song on her bird-shaped flute.

HEART'S DESIRE

Palace of the Governors

This is a day I'll remember as long as I live, thought Josefina. She was holding Tía Dolores's hand, and she gave it a squeeze. Tía Dolores smiled down at Josefina's glowing, upturned face. "Any minute now," Tía Dolores said. They were standing in a crowd that had gathered in front of the Palace of the Governors in Santa Fe. Everyone was waiting, waiting, *waiting* for the wagon train to pull into town. *Any minute now,* thought Josefina with a delighted shiver. *Any minute!*

Soon after dawn while the air was still cool, Josefina and her family and one of Abuelita's servants had walked into Santa Fe. Abuelita had stayed home because she didn't like crowds. But everyone else was eager to join the people gathering to see the wagon train. All along the road, they saw tents that had sprung up overnight. Indians had come with pottery and blankets and horses to trade. Fur trappers had come down from the mountains. Soldiers had come from their fort up on the hill. People had come from villages and ranchos for miles around. They all gathered in the *plaza* that was in the center of Santa Fe. Even the long, low *adobe* buildings built around all four sides of the plaza seemed to lean forward expectantly, looking for the wagon train.

Josefina had never seen so many people! Words in different languages swirled around her in a confused jumble, until suddenly she heard one shout above the others.

"The wagons! The americanos! The wagon train is here!" someone called out. Then many voices rose up together in a roar. Church bells rang. Josefina's heart was pounding. She called out with the others, "The wagon train is here!"

Around Josefina, many people were clapping, cheering, and waving as the americanos' wagons lumbered into view. But other people were not so enthusiastic. They stood quietly, arms crossed over their chests, watching the wagons with questioning looks, as if they were not convinced that the arrival of the americanos was a good thing. Josefina stood on tiptoe to see the wagons better. But she didn't let go of Tía Dolores's hand, and she was glad to be safely wedged between Tía Dolores and Papá. The wagons were so heavy they rumbled like the thunder of an oncoming storm and made the earth shake under Josefina's feet.

The americanos driving the wagons whooped and hooted and whistled and threw their hats into the air. They circled their whips and then snapped them so that they made a *pop!* as loud as a gunshot. Wagon after wagon rolled into the plaza. Josefina counted more than twenty. Some were pulled by plodding oxen who seemed half asleep in spite of all the noise. But most of the wagons were pulled by mules that pricked up their ears and looked pleased at all the attention.

"Tía Dolores," said Josefina. "Look how big the wagons are!"

The wagons *were* enormous. Their wheels
stood higher than Josefina's head! Some of the
wagons were flying a flag different from the
Mexican flag Josefina was used to. This flag
was red, white, and blue. The flag's stripes
and stars looked snappy and clean in the
bright sunshine. Josefina thought the
americanos looked cleaned up, too, as if
that morning they'd scrubbed their faces, slicked
down their hair, put on their Sunday-best clothes,
and polished the dust of hundreds of miles off their
boots. Some of the men looked rough, while others
looked quiet and well mannered. But to Josefina's
eyes, *all* the americanos looked glad to be in Santa Fe
and at the end of the trail at last.

Papá bent his head toward Tía Dolores so she
could hear him above the hubbub. "Your father and
I are going to look for Señor Patrick at the customs
house," he said. "The americanos have to go there
to make a list of their goods and to pay taxes. The
servant will stay with you and the girls."

Tía Dolores nodded. "Very well," she said. "Go
ahead."

But Papá didn't go. His eyes had a twinkle in

19

them as he looked at Tía Dolores. "Have you told
the girls?" he asked her.

"Not yet," answered Tía Dolores.

"Told us what?" asked Francisca immediately.

Papá laughed. "Tell them," he said to Tía Dolores.
"After all, it was your idea. We wouldn't have as
much to trade today if it were not for you." His
voice was full of gratitude and affection. Tía Dolores
smiled, and then Papá went off with Abuelito to
find Patrick.

"Please, Tía Dolores! Tell us what Papá meant!"
begged the sisters.

Tía Dolores's eyes were shining. "Your papá
and I think that you girls deserve something for
all the hard work you've done weaving," she said.
"We've decided that you may each choose one of
the blankets you wove, and you may sell it or trade
it for anything you wish."

"*Oh!*" gasped Francisca and Clara. "How
wonderful!"

Josefina didn't say anything. Instead, she
hugged Tía Dolores. It had been Tía Dolores's idea
to weave blankets for Papá to trade for sheep.
Josefina and her sisters had never expected to use

the blankets they'd woven to get anything for themselves. *It's just like Tía Dolores to think of something so generous,* thought Josefina.

"Well!" said Francisca. She had an eager gleam in her eyes. "We'd better look around and decide what we'll get with our blankets."

There was certainly much to see! Tía Dolores and the sisters walked slowly around the plaza to watch the americanos unload their wagons. Some of the americanos had rented small stores to display their wares. Others had wooden stalls or spaces on the street where they set out their goods. Never in her life had Josefina imagined such a variety of things. She saw bolts of brightly colored cottons, wools, and silks. There were veils, shawls, sashes, and ribbons. There were shoes and hats, boots and stockings, combs, brushes, toothbrushes, and even silver toothpicks!

Clara stood for a long time studying pots and pans until Francisca dragged her away to look at buttons and jewelry she saw sparkling ahead. Clara stopped halfway there to gaze at knitting needles. Tía Dolores was distracted by some books, and the girls were fascinated by the mirrors that reflected their delighted faces. Many people were crowded around the watches and clocks, and even more were crowded around the tools. A few people were paying for the americanos' goods with silver coins, but most people were trading or swapping. Josefina saw a man from the pueblo swap a beautiful pottery jar he'd made for an americano's glass bottle. A fur trapper traded a bear skin for a hunting knife.

There were so many things, Josefina didn't know how she'd ever choose something for herself. Then Tía Dolores and the girls stopped in front of a trader who had toys among his goods. One toy in particular caught Josefina's eye. It was a little toy farm carved out of wood.

"Oh, look!" said Josefina as she knelt in front of it. There was a tiny cow, a horse pulling a cart, a goat, and a funny pink pig standing in front of a white stable. Two green trees shaded a painted house with a white fence behind it.

"You can almost hear the cow moo, can't you?" someone joked. It was Patrick. He and Papá and Abuelito had finished their business and had come to find Tía Dolores and the girls.

*There were so many things, Josefina didn't know how she'd
ever choose something for herself.*

"That reminds me of how the farms look back home in Missouri."

Josefina imagined what it would be like to sit in the shade of the two green trees or climb on the white fence. "I wish I could magically shrink," she said to Patrick. "I'd like to go inside the house. I've never seen a house that's so straight up and down, with such a steep roof and so many big windows!"

"It's different, isn't it?" said Patrick. "Here in New Mexico your houses are low. They look like they grew right up out of the ground because they're made out of earth, and they don't have any sharp corners. Where I come from the buildings seem to want to stick up and call attention to themselves. Sort of like the people, I guess!"

"I think the farm is very pretty," said Josefina. "I like it."

Clara looked over Josefina's shoulder. "But it's just a toy, Josefina," she said. "You shouldn't waste your blanket on *that!*"

Josefina sighed. Clara was being sensible, as usual. But Josefina couldn't help wanting the farm. She was sure it would be fun to play with the pink pig! And knowing that the little farm reminded

Patrick of his home made Josefina like it even more.

Papá looped his finger around one of Josefina's braids and moved the braid behind her ear. Then he stooped and spoke softly so that only Josefina could hear. "We'll come back," he said kindly. "And you can look at the toy farm again." Josefina looked into his understanding brown eyes. "If that's what you want, then that's what you should get," Papá said. "Don't let anyone talk you out of your heart's desire."

Papá took Josefina's hand and stood up straight. Then in a louder voice he said to Tía Dolores, "I have good news. Señor Patrick has found traders who want to buy all of our mules."

"Oh?" said Tía Dolores. Her eyes had a question in them.

"Sí," answered Papá. His voice was serious and sure. "I have decided to let Señor Patrick trade the mules for us. He knows the americano traders. He can speak English to them. And he has promised to get me a good price."

"My friends will be glad to get the mules," said Patrick quickly. "Mules are sturdy. They do better than oxen on the wagon trails. Oxen are fussy eaters. They have delicate feet, and they get sunburned."

Patrick pointed to his own red nose and joked, "Just like me!" Everyone laughed, and Patrick went on. "I can get you silver for the mules," he said.

Silver! This was lucky indeed. Normally, Papá would have traded the mules for goods from the americanos. Then he would trade the goods for sheep. Josefina knew Papá must be pleased. It would be much easier to buy the sheep they needed with silver.

"Señor Montoya, may I come by later today to get the mules?" Patrick asked Papá. "I can bring some of your silver today, and the rest at the end of the week after I've sold all of the mules."

"Very well," said Papá. "I know I can trust you to keep your word." He and Patrick shook hands to seal their agreement. Josefina saw that Papá's grasp was firm. *Oh, I am so glad Papá has decided to trust Señor Patrick*, thought Josefina.

Abuelito seemed glad, too. "When you come for the mules, you must stay for dinner," he said to Patrick. "We'll celebrate!"

"And please remember to bring your violin," said Tía Dolores. "We can't celebrate without music!"

"I'll remember," said Patrick. He said *adiós* to everyone. Then he strolled away, cheerfully whistling Josefina's bird song.

CHAPTER
THREE
—

A CHARM FROM THE SKY

Later that afternoon, Patrick came to
Abuelito's rancho to get Papá's mules.
He was going to take them back to
Santa Fe after dinner. Josefina had climbed to her
hilltop to meet him and lead him to the house.

Before they started down the hill, Patrick tilted his
head back and said, "I've never seen a sky so blue."

"Mamá used to say the sky is that blue because
it's the bottom of heaven," said Josefina.

Patrick smiled. He pulled a small brass telescope
out of his coat pocket. As Josefina watched, he
focused the telescope on a point to the southeast.
"Look through there," he said as he handed her the
telescope.

Josefina focused the telescope for herself.
"I see San Miguel Chapel," she said. She recognized
the church easily even though it was far away. It
came clearly into view through the telescope, as if
someone had painted a perfect picture of it in a tiny
round frame.

"Well," said Patrick, "yesterday I climbed up to
the bell of San Miguel Chapel. While I was up there
a little bit of the sky fell off, right into my hand. See?"

Josefina giggled when she looked.
Patrick held a small chunk of turquoise
in his hand. The turquoise *was* the same
glorious blue as the sky.

Patrick tossed the chunk of turquoise up in the
air, caught it with the same hand, and put it in his
pocket. "Now I'll have a little bit of New Mexican
sky with me even when I go back home," he said,
patting his pocket as if he had a treasure in it. Then
he pretended to frown. "What's this?" he asked.
He pulled a sheet of paper out of the same pocket,
unfolded it, and then handed it to Josefina with a
grin. "I believe this is for you, Señorita Josefina."

"Gracias!" said Josefina. The paper was
sheet music. It had the notes and the words to

a song printed on it. Josefina couldn't read the words because they were in English.

She didn't know how to read the notes, either, which were lined up like orderly black birds on straight black branches. But she had seen sheet music before. Tía Dolores had some. "Perhaps when we go home, Tía Dolores will teach me to play this song on the piano," Josefina said to Patrick. "She knows how to read music. I think Papá does, too, unless he's forgotten." Josefina hesitated, then said, "Papá used to play the violin."

"Did he?" asked Patrick.

"Sí," said Josefina. She looked down at the sheet music and said quietly, "He used to play when Mamá was alive. But when . . . when she died, he gave his violin away. I think he was just too sad to play it anymore. We were all too sad for music for a long, long time." Josefina looked up at Patrick. "It's been better since Tía Dolores came to stay with us. We've all been happier, especially Papá. And Tía Dolores loves music. She even brought her piano with her when she came up the Camino Real from Mexico City with Abuelito's caravan. You should hear Abuelito tell *that* story!"

30

"He promised to tell me some of his adventures," said Patrick as they headed down the hill to the house. "If I ask, do you think he'll tell me the piano story this evening?"

"With pleasure!" answered Josefina. She knew there was nothing in the world Abuelito liked better than telling a story!

It was with *great* pleasure that Abuelito told the piano story and many other stories about the Camino Real during dinner. Then Patrick told stories about the Santa Fe Trail. He talked about herds of buffalo so endless they made the plains look black, and rivers so wide you could not see across them.

After dinner, Patrick took out his violin. He played such lively tunes that he soon had everyone clapping their hands and tapping their feet. The sun set and the fire was lit, but the moon poured so much silvery light into the room that they didn't need to light candles. Patrick's music was merry and lighthearted, full of fancy, funny twists and turns. Abuelito kept time slapping

31

his leg, and Abuelita's dangling earrings swung and sparkled as she nodded her head to the rhythm of the music.

Patrick played and played. He was right in the middle of a song when, in one smooth movement, before anyone realized what he was doing, he handed his violin to Papá, saying, "Now it's your turn, Señor Montoya."

Suddenly, the room was completely quiet.

What is Señor Patrick doing? worried Josefina. *I told him Papá didn't play anymore!*

But Papá did not frown. Slowly, as if he were both eager and reluctant at the same time, Papá tucked Patrick's violin under his chin. He held the slender neck of the violin in his broad hand and delicately ran the bow over the strings. Chills ran up and down Josefina's spine.

"What shall I play?" Papá asked.

No one answered.

Josefina hopped up and put the sheet music Patrick had given her in front of Papá. "Play this, Papá," she said.

Papá began to play. He played softly at first, but every note became surer. Then Patrick began to sing the words. His voice was husky and low. Though Josefina could not understand the English words he was singing, she understood the wistful feeling of the song. Patrick sang:

> *'Mid pleasure and palaces though we may roam,*
> *Be it ever so humble there's no place like home.*
> *A charm from the skies seems to hallow us there,*
> *Which, seek through the world is ne'er met with*
>   *elsewhere.*

Patrick stopped singing. But Papá continued to play, making up a song that blended Patrick's song with an old Spanish song. Josefina sat still, listening intently, with her eyes fixed on Papá's face. Josefina knew that Papá's song was telling a story full of longing and hope.

Josefina wished the music would never end. Tía Dolores must have felt the same way. As the last note faded, she sighed a sigh that seemed to come straight from her heart. "Oh," she said to Papá. "That was lovely!"

Papá handed the violin back to Patrick, then smiled at Tía Dolores.

In that moment, Josefina knew what she wanted

*Josefina knew that Papá's song was
telling a story full of longing and hope.*

to trade for her blanket. She knew without a doubt what her heart's desire was.

She wanted Patrick's violin for Papá.

"No."

It was much later. Patrick had left, taking Papá's mules with him.

"No," said Clara again. She and Josefina and Francisca were in the sleeping sala they shared. All three were sitting on the bed Josefina and Clara slept in. But the sisters weren't even close to sleeping. They were having an argument. "I won't," said Clara flatly. "It's just not sensible."

Josefina and Francisca shared an exasperated look.

"But Clara," pleaded Francisca, who had agreed with Josefina's plan right away. "We need your blanket, too. It will work only if we all do it. Patrick's violin is worth at *least* three blankets."

"How about Ana's blanket?" asked Clara.

"We couldn't use it without asking her," said Josefina. "Anyway, Tía Dolores is going to trade it for boots for Ana's little boys."

"I want to trade my blanket for something practical, too!" said Clara. "It's different for you. You want that silly toy farm, and Francisca wants a mirror, which is just a luxury. I want useful things like knitting needles."

"Clara," coaxed Francisca. "When we go home, I will give you all of my knitting needles. I promise. They're good as new."

"Because you never use them!" said Clara. "Besides, I could get lots more than knitting needles. The americanos pay well for woven blankets."

Francisca started to say something sharp, but Josefina spoke first. "Didn't you see how happy Papá looked while he was playing Señor Patrick's violin?" Josefina asked Clara. "We have to get it for him. We just have to."

"Señor Patrick will probably say no anyway," said Clara stubbornly.

But Josefina could be stubborn, too. "We've got to at least *ask* him," she said. She looked straight into Clara's eyes and said something she *knew* would convince her to cooperate. "The truth is, it isn't only Papá's happiness I'm thinking of. You must have seen how much Tía Dolores loved it when Papá played. She's been so kind to us. Don't you think we owe it to her to please her if we can? Think how happy she would be at home if Papá played the violin while she played her piano."

Clara groaned and flopped facedown on the bed. But Josefina knew that by now she was only pretending to be cross. "Oh, all right!" Clara said, her voice muffled. "I'll do it! May God forgive me for being so foolish!"

Josefina and Francisca smiled at each other in triumph. They knew Clara couldn't refuse a chance to make Papá *and* Tía Dolores happy.

The next afternoon, the sun shone down straight and strong. It baked out the spicy scent of the *piñón* trees as the sisters and Tía Dolores walked to the plaza. A servant was with them because it wasn't safe while the traders were in town for ladies to go there without a man to protect them. The servant stayed with the sisters while Tía Dolores stepped inside a shop to trade Ana's blanket for boots.

piñón

Patrick soon came up to the sisters to say hello.

Even though it was very hot, Clara had been clutching her blanket tightly to her chest. But she handed it over without a murmur when Josefina and Francisca gave their blankets to Patrick.

"These are beautiful," said Patrick. "And they are worth a great deal. Why are you giving them to me?"

Josefina took a deep breath. "We were wondering if you would consider taking them in trade for your—for your violin," she said all in a rush. That's what she said aloud. Inside she was praying, *Please let Señor Patrick say yes.*

Patrick looked surprised. "But I thought you wanted the little farm," he said to Josefina. "And you told me you wanted a mirror, Señorita Francisca. And you wanted knitting needles, Señorita Clara. You could get those things and more with these blankets."

"We *all* want the violin more than anything else," Josefina said firmly. "We want it for Papá."

"Ah!" said Patrick. He looked at the blankets and ran his hand over them. At last he said, "Your papá is very lucky to have daughters who love him so much. I'd be honored to trade my violin for blankets made by such good-hearted girls as you."

"Oh, gracias, Señor Patrick!" said Josefina with a huge smile.

"It's I who must thank you for these soft blankets," Patrick said. Then he added with a chuckle, "That violin isn't very comfortable to sleep on!"

Josefina laughed and Patrick went on to say, "Meet me here tomorrow afternoon at this same time. I'll give you the violin then."

"We'll be here!" promised Josefina and Francisca.

As Patrick walked away with their blankets, Clara shook her head. "I hope we can trust him," she said.

"Of course we can!" said Francisca stoutly. "Papá trusted him with the mules, didn't he?"

But Clara couldn't answer because Tía Dolores had returned. "Why, girls," she asked, "where are your blankets?"

"I hope you don't mind," said Francisca. "We traded them already."

Tía Dolores smiled. "What did you get?"

"Well," said Josefina. "We . . . it's . . ." Finally

she gave up and grinned at her aunt. "We really can't say," she explained. "But you'll see tomorrow."

Tía Dolores laughed. "How nice!" she said. "You'll surprise me!"

"We certainly will," said Clara with a sigh.

But Josefina knew Clara was as excited about their surprise as she and Francisca were. Josefina was having a hard time hiding her own excitement. Her thoughts raced ahead to the next day. She couldn't *wait* to get the violin for Papá. She hoped the hours would fly by until it was time to meet Patrick!

Though it was raining hard the next afternoon, the three sisters went to the plaza with a servant to meet Patrick. They stood exactly where he had told them to be. They pulled their *rebozos* over their heads and hunched their shoulders against the rain. Hour after hour after hour the girls waited. By the time the bell in San Miguel Chapel rang for six o'clock prayers, their skirts were drenched and their shoes were sopping. It was clear that the servant was sorry he had come and was eager to go home where it was warm and dry. Josefina couldn't blame him. A gust of wind drove rain into her face so that it was as wet as if she had been crying.

"What shall we do?" asked Francisca. A strand of her hair was stuck flat against her cheek.

Clara shivered. "Let's go *home*," she said. "We've waited three hours. Señor Patrick is not coming. That's all. He's just not going to come."

"Maybe he forgot," said Josefina. "Maybe we misunderstood. Maybe we were supposed to come tomorrow."

"Maybe!" exclaimed Clara. "You can *maybe* all you want, but I'm going home right now! Abuelita will be worried sick about us."

"Wait!" said Josefina. She saw a man she knew was a friend of Patrick's. She gathered up all her courage and hurried to him. Clara and Francisca followed close behind. "Excuse me, señor," Josefina said. "Do you know where Señor Patrick O'Toole is?"

"Patrick O'Toole?" said the man. "He's gone."

Josefina's heart dropped. "But . . . but he was supposed to meet us here," she said. "There must be some mistake."

The man shrugged. "O'Toole's a scout," he said. "Last night, the captain of the wagon train told the scouts to head out for the Camino Real. By now they're long gone." The man nodded a brisk good-bye, then rushed off in the rain.

Gone! The word echoed inside Josefina's head. She felt as if she were in a cold, cruel nightmare. She stood numbly, too confused and miserable to talk.

Francisca was silent, too. But Clara had a lot to say. "I knew we shouldn't have trusted that Señor Patrick," she said furiously. "You know what this means, don't you? Señor Patrick has cheated us, so I'm sure he's cheated Papá, too! We've lost our blankets, but Papá has probably lost all the mules! We've got to get home to tell him."

"That's enough, Clara," said Francisca, her voice tired. She slid her arm around Josefina's shoulders. "Let's go."

Homeward the girls trudged. The wind swirled the rain around them. Josefina hardly noticed. She could think only of Patrick. With all her heart, she wanted to hold on to her trust in him. But it certainly seemed that Clara was right and that Patrick had lied to them all.

As they passed the toy trader, Josefina peered out from under her dripping rebozo and saw that the toy farm was gone. *Not that it matters*, Josefina thought sadly. *Now I have nothing to trade for it anyway.* But that was only a tiny disappointment compared to what Patrick seemed to have done. *Oh, Señor Patrick*, thought Josefina. *How could you betray us like this?*

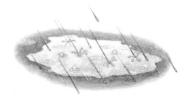

SHINING LIKE HOPE

Papá and Abuelito had gone to trade blankets for tools and did not come home until it was time for dinner. As soon as they walked in the door, Clara rushed to Papá. "Something terrible has happened," Clara said. "Señor Patrick is gone!"

"Gone?" gasped Abuelito. "But he hasn't paid your papá the rest of the silver he owes him. He promised—"

"Señor O'Toole's promises are lies," said Clara. "Yesterday Francisca, Josefina, and I gave him our blankets. He was supposed to meet us today to give us something in return for them. But he took our blankets and left! He stole them!" Clara looked at

44

Papá and said, "He cheated us, so I'm certain he's cheated you, too."

"I knew it was a mistake to trust that americano!" said Abuelita. "He used his jokes and flattery and music to trick us into liking him! We didn't really know him at all!" She turned to Papá. "If you go to town right now, perhaps you can find your mules and get them back," she said.

Papá's face looked hard as stone.

Tía Dolores spoke carefully. "It's still possible that this is just a misunderstanding," she said. "If you reclaim your mules, you'll be saying that Señor Patrick is dishonest. If you're wrong, you'll shame him and yourself. You'll ruin his good name and your own as well."

"Sí," said Abuelito. "The other americanos won't want to trade with you and you'll get nothing for your mules this year. You'd better be sure—"

"Sure?" interrupted Abuelita. "How much more sure could anyone be?" She spoke to Papá with urgency. "Señor O'Toole stole from your daughters. If he'd stoop to that, you can be sure he stole from you, too! Go now, get your mules back before the rest of the americanos leave, before it's too late!"

Papá was a wise man who did not act hastily. He thought for a long moment. Then he spoke in a sad, tired voice. "It seems I have been wrong to trust young Señor O'Toole," he said. "I don't want to ruin my chances of trading with the other americanos, but I can't risk losing twenty good mules. I must do what I can to get them back."

"Sí!" began Abuelita. "Go—"

But Papá held up his hand. "It's useless to go now," he said. "It will be impossible to find the mules in the dark. I'll go tomorrow, at first light."

Abuelita pressed her lips into a thin, worried line and said no more. No one had any more to say. Soon after dinner, they all went to bed.

But Josefina was too miserable to sleep. For hours she lay awake, staring out of the narrow window. Finally she gave up. She rose, dressed, slipped outside, and climbed the hilltop behind the house.

The rain had washed the air clean, and the full moon was bright, shining like hope in the sky. Suddenly, out of the corner of her eye, Josefina saw a shadow move. "Señor Patrick?" she whispered, thinking wildly that he had come to find her.

But no. It was only an old tortoise making its
way patiently across the sandy ground. Josefina
sighed, and watched the tortoise stop under a piñón
tree. Oddly, the ground looked white there.
Josefina looked again. The ground wasn't
white. Someone had left a piece of paper
under the tree. Josefina bent down to look
at the paper and gasped. *On top of the paper she saw
Patrick's chunk of turquoise!*

With trembling hands, Josefina picked
up the turquoise and the paper. She
unfolded the paper carefully, knowing that
Patrick must have left it for her. It was soggy
from being in the rain. The ink had run so much that
the drawing was blurry. When Josefina held it up so
that the moon shone on it, she could see that it was a
drawing of a church. But which church? There were
five in Santa Fe.

Was this one of Patrick's jokes? Josefina looked
at the chunk of turquoise and remembered how
Patrick had joked that it was a piece of the sky that
fell into his hand when he climbed to the top of . . .
Oh! Josefina pulled in her breath. San Miguel
Chapel! That was it! Patrick had left the chunk of

turquoise on top of the paper so that she would know that the drawing was San Miguel Chapel. Josefina's heart skipped a beat. That was where the violin was! Josefina squeezed her fist shut around the piece of turquoise. *Oh, Señor Patrick!* she thought. *Forgive me for thinking that you lied.*

Josefina slipped and slid down the rain-slick hill, tripping over her own feet in her hurry. She crossed the courtyard and burst into the room she shared with Francisca and Clara. "Wake up!" she hissed, shaking her sisters' shoulders. When they opened their eyes, Josefina waved the drawing at them and said, "Señor Patrick didn't lie! He left this to tell me where the violin is." She swallowed to catch her breath. "He left the violin in San Miguel Chapel."

"Let me see that," said Francisca. She lit a candle and took the drawing.

Clara looked bewildered. "But why . . ." she began.

"Señor Patrick put the violin in San Miguel Chapel because he knew it would be safe there," explained Josefina. "He had to leave Santa Fe in the middle of the night. He couldn't bring the violin here and wake up the whole household. He couldn't leave it up on the hilltop where it would be ruined by rain. He couldn't write a note to tell us where it was because we can't read English and he can't write Spanish. So he left me the drawing and his chunk of turquoise. He trusted me to figure it out." Josefina took the paper back from Francisca. "I'll show this to Papá, and it will prove to him that Señor Patrick is honest. Papá won't have to break off the trade!"

"Don't bother Papá with that! It's just a piece of paper," said Clara. "It doesn't prove anything. Only the violin would prove that Señor Patrick didn't cheat us—and Papá, too."

"Then I'll have to *get* the violin, won't I?" said Josefina. "I'll go now."

Clara was horrified. "Josefina!" she sputtered. "You can't go into Santa Fe by yourself in the middle of the night! It's dangerous. The traders drink too much. They gamble and fight and shoot off their guns." She shuddered. "You can't go."

"Not by yourself," said Francisca. She stood up and began to pull on her clothes. "I'll go with you."

"Oh, gracias, Francisca!" said Josefina. "We'll have to hurry. It'll be sunrise in a few hours. We've got to get the violin before Papá goes to town to take his mules back." She looked at Clara. "You must promise you won't tell anyone that we've gone."

"I promise," said Clara. "But *you* must promise to be careful. I'll pray for you." She sighed. "If only I'd traded my blanket for those knitting needles!"

Josefina and Francisca crept from their room, tiptoed across the courtyard, and slid out the front gate. They sidled along the outside wall of the house. Then they darted to the kitchen garden and crouched behind its stick fence to catch their breath.

In a moment, Francisca touched Josefina's shoulder and then pointed toward the road. Josefina nodded. Both girls sprang forward, dashed to the road, and ran down it as fast as they could. With every step, the lantern she'd brought banged against Josefina's leg. Soon her arm ached from carrying it. Her stomach was in a knot, and her chest was burning because she was out of breath. But she kept on. Francisca was right by her side.

Soon light shining from windows and doorways spilled across the road. The girls heard bursts of music and clapping and the thunder of dancing feet coming from *fandangos* and parties. "We'll have to stay away from the plaza," whispered Josefina as she and Francisca skittered down a narrow lane. "Too many people."

Francisca nodded. "Let's—" she began.

But just at that moment, the girls heard voices. A group of men swayed toward them, singing and laughing and all talking at once.

Quickly, Josefina and Francisca shrank into a doorway, pushing themselves flat against the door, holding their breath. Josefina's heart was pounding so loudly, she felt sure the men would hear it! But the rowdy men lurched by the girls' hiding place. Their voices filled the lane and then faded as they moved farther away. When she thought the men were gone, Josefina lifted her lantern and cautiously looked out to see if anyone else was coming. When she didn't see anyone, she signaled to Francisca to follow her.

But the moment the girls stepped out of the doorway, a rough voice frightened them. "What have we here?" said the voice. It belonged to a tall man who loomed toward them out of the darkness. "Two señoritas!" growled the man. He stepped forward, but Josefina tripped him, and he fell with a heavy thud. Josefina took hold of Francisca's hand and the two girls ran for all they were worth, not caring where they went as long as it was *away*.

Like birds of the night, Josefina and Francisca darted from shadow to shadow, skirting the center of town and never stopping. Just when Josefina thought she could not run another step, the moon-washed front of San Miguel Chapel rose up before them into the dark night sky. Up the steps they flew. Josefina grasped the handle of one of the huge

"What have we here?" said the rough voice.

doors with both hands and pulled it with all her strength. Slowly, the door creaked open and the two breathless girls ran inside.

Trembling, the girls walked forward. It was cold inside the church, and at first it seemed darker than outside. Josefina's lantern made only a small circle of light around her feet. But as her eyes adjusted, Josefina saw candles placed in a cluster on the floor in front of the altar where people had lit them and left them as a kind of prayer. The candles shone like stars fallen from the sky. With careful steps, Josefina and Francisca walked toward them.

Suddenly, Josefina's heart soared up with happiness. For there, safely placed against the wall by a small altar, was Patrick's violin in its case. *God bless you, Señor Patrick!* Josefina thought. She grabbed Francisca's hand and pulled her over to the violin. "Look!" she breathed. Patrick had even tied a ribbon around the violin case. Josefina knelt down and grinned. "I think Señor Patrick knew that you would come with me," she said to Francisca. Because next to the violin was the mirror that

Francisca had wanted to get with her blanket.

Francisca smiled her beautiful smile. "He left something for you, too," she said. She picked up a small box and handed it to Josefina.

Josefina looked inside, and the first thing she saw was the funny pink pig. It was the little farm! All of the pieces fit together neatly in the small box. Josefina touched the farmhouse. *Gracias, Señor Patrick,* she thought. *I promise I will remember you every time I play with the little farm.*

"We'd better go," said Francisca.

The girls stood. When Josefina picked up the violin, something poked her hand. Josefina looked. Patrick had used the ribbon to tie knitting needles for Clara to the back of the violin case!

Josefina and Francisca glanced at each other and smiled. But there was no time to lose. When the girls walked outside the church, a thin streak of gray above the mountains was already hinting that the sun would soon rise. Josefina knew that meant Papá was probably awake and getting ready to come into town. She and Francisca had to get home fast. They had to stop him!

Though they were tired, Josefina and Francisca pushed themselves homeward as fast as they could go. The road home had never been so long.

As they ran toward Abuelito's house, they saw that they were just in time. Papá and Tía Dolores were standing together. Papá's horse was saddled, and he was just about to mount up to ride into town.

Josefina didn't hesitate. She ran straight to Papá and held out the violin. "Look, Papá," she said, all out of breath. "This is Señor Patrick's violin. This is what we traded our blankets for. He didn't lie to us. He left the violin for us in the church. Please don't go into town! Please don't take back your mules. Señor Patrick is honest. The violin proves it!" She thrust the violin into Papá's hands. "If he kept his promise to us, then surely he'll keep his promise to you."

Papá was astounded. He looked at the violin and then at his two daughters.

Tía Dolores was the first to speak. "Do you mean to say that you two—" She broke off, as if the rest of her question were too unbelievable to ask. "You two went into Santa Fe by yourselves in the middle of the night to get this violin?"

Josefina and Francisca nodded. "We're sorry," said Josefina.

"But we had to prove to Papá that Señor Patrick is honest," Francisca added.

They all looked at Papá. "You stopped me from making a serious mistake, and I am grateful," he said in his deep and deliberate voice. "Now I am sure that somehow Señor Patrick will get me the money he owes me for the mules." He paused, then said, "Go inside. Your abuelita will have some sharp words to say to you when she finds out what you have done, and I . . ."

The girls hung their heads. They knew they deserved the scolding they expected. But all Papá said was, "I must ask a servant to unsaddle my horse. It seems I won't be going to town this morning after all."

Francisca and Josefina glanced at each other. Wasn't Papá going to scold them any more than that? They didn't wait to see, but turned to go inside.

"Wait!" said Papá. He held the violin out to Josefina. "Take your violin."

"Oh!" said Josefina. "The violin isn't for us. It's for you, Papá."

"For me?" Papá asked. "Why?"

"Because," said Josefina, "it made you and Tía Dolores happy."

Papá looked at Tía Dolores, and Josefina saw something that *might* have been a smile pass between them.

That evening, a friend of Patrick's brought the rest of the silver to Papá. Josefina and Francisca only had a peek at the man as he was leaving after dinner. They'd had to spend the day in their room as punishment for sneaking into town. Abuelita said that they should pray for God's forgiveness and everyone else's as well. But then she hugged both sisters, so Josefina thought she wasn't *too* angry. Clara was so delighted with her new knitting needles she kept Josefina and Francisca company and knit all day. Francisca amused them by using her mirror to make reflected sunlight dance on the walls and flit across their skirts like tiny gold birds. Josefina spent the time quietly playing with her toy farm. And so the day passed peacefully.

Josefina was tired after her adventure. She went
to bed early and fell into a dreamless sleep.

Something woke her in the middle of the night.
It wasn't the moon, because the sky was cloudy.
Josefina got out of bed and opened the door to feel
the cool night breeze on her cheeks. A sound nearly
too soft to be heard drifted on the breeze. Josefina
had to hold her breath to hear it. She almost wasn't
sure what the sound was. When she realized, she
smiled. Papá was gently, very gently, playing an
old Spanish song on his violin.

The breeze blew the clouds away, and suddenly
the courtyard was full of moonlight. Josefina saw
that she was not the only one awake and listening
to Papá. Standing in the doorway to her room,
humming Papá's song, was Tía Dolores.

A PEEK INTO
THE PAST

Grasses and short, hardy trees grow in the high, mountainous desert of New Mexico.

In the 1820s, the New Mexico landscape was harsh and beautiful—just as it is today. From Josefina's home, dry, tawny hills rolled off for miles in all directions, dotted with desert bushes and scrubby *piñón* trees. To the east, pine-covered mountains rose up, capped with snow in the winter. When the mountain snow melted in spring, it flowed down in cold streams, bringing precious water to the parched land below. These streams made it possible for Indians and Spanish settlers to grow crops.

The dry air was so clear that Josefina could see for fifty miles or more, and sounds carried far in the desert stillness. Most days, the sky was a deep, clear blue.

In late summer, huge rain clouds built up over the mountains each afternoon. Sometimes showers fell, but often the rain evaporated before it reached the ground.

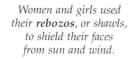

At night, the vast sky shimmered with stars.

In Josefina's time, people spent much of their lives outdoors. Nearly all New Mexicans farmed, which meant long hours tending animals, fields, and gardens. Women did many household tasks outside, too, including baking and laundry.

New Mexican towns and villages were built around an open square called a *plaza*. People gathered outside in the plaza to talk, conduct business, and work. Community celebrations were also held in the plaza. On holidays, people gathered there for religious processions and festive community meals. Sometimes local musicians, poets, and actors performed in the plaza, too.

*Women and girls used their **rebozos**, or shawls, to shield their faces from sun and wind.*

In Josefina's time, travel was difficult and dangerous, so people did not take vacations for fun. But New Mexicans did travel for other reasons. Families traveled long distances by horse or wagon to

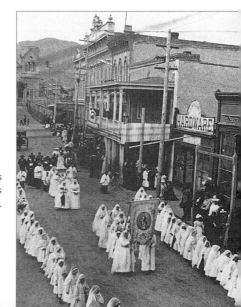

*Community activities often took place in a town's **plaza**, or central square. This photo from the 1890s shows a religious procession in Santa Fe's plaza.*

In large towns, like this Mexican city, plazas were busy marketplaces where people came to buy, sell, and trade.

visit relatives, especially for important events like weddings. Visits like these lasted for days and were times of great celebration.

Trading was also an important reason to travel. Once or twice a year, families like the Montoyas might go to bigger towns or special fairs to trade their wool, weaving, crops, or animals for items they could not grow or make at home. Trading trips were opportunities for families to get things they needed, and—just as important—to see old friends and catch up on news.

When Josefina was a girl, the most exciting place she could have visited was the capital city of Santa Fe. Although it was small compared to cities today, Santa Fe was the biggest town for hundreds of miles around.

Its plaza was the most important marketplace in all of New Mexico.

For visitors like Josefina, Santa Fe's plaza held marvelous sights and a fascinating mix of people.

In the capital city of Santa Fe, the narrow streets bustled with people and activity.

Local merchants sold fine cloth, ribbons, spices, mirrors, jewelry, shoes, books, cones of brown sugar, and much more. Pueblo Indians from nearby villages came with pottery, blankets, baskets, chiles, and other foods to trade. Bands of Indians from distant tribes such as the Comanche and Apache might trade hides and buffalo skins. Sometimes a French trapper arrived with loads of valuable beaver pelts. And by 1824, there was a new kind of trader in the plaza—American men bringing wagon trains full of goods from the United States. Just think of the many languages Josefina might have heard in the plaza all at once—Spanish, French, Comanche, Apache, Pueblo Indian languages, and English!

In Santa Fe, people could buy goods from all over the world— fancy shoes and jars from Mexico City (top), pottery and baskets from local Indians (middle), bonnets and glass bottles from the United States.

*Wild-looking **mountain men**, like this French trapper, came to Santa Fe with furs to trade.*

American trade in Santa Fe began in the autumn of 1821, just after Mexico won its independence from Spain. For the first time, foreign traders were allowed to do business in New Mexico. Soon, more and more Americans were coming to Santa Fe each summer with wagon loads of goods to trade. The rugged route

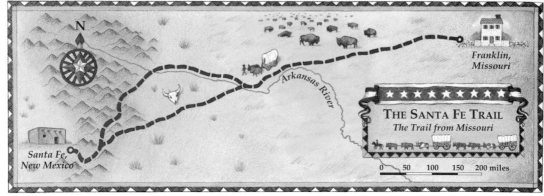

Franklin,
Missouri

Arkansas River

THE SANTA FE TRAIL
The Trail from Missouri

0   50   100   150   200 miles

Santa Fe,
New Mexico

Americans began traveling the Santa Fe Trail in 1821, when Josefina was a girl. The trail passed through the present-day states of Missouri, Kansas, Colorado, and New Mexico.

they used became known as the Santa Fe Trail. It began in Missouri and crossed more than 800 miles of bone-dry plains and high, treacherous mountains. From Santa Fe, American wagon trains often continued south along the *Camino Real* to trade in large Mexican cities. Like Patrick, some American traders learned to speak Spanish so they could conduct business with New Mexicans.

Some New Mexicans didn't trust the Americans, but others welcomed the new traders. American goods cost much less than items carried up the Camino Real from Mexico. And Americans brought new items that quickly became popular, such as calico cloth and machine-made

An American wagon train on the Santa Fe Trail. The dangerous trip from Missouri to New Mexico often took three months or more.

66

clothing and shoes. In return for American goods, New Mexicans traded mules, handwoven wool blankets, and gold or silver Spanish coins. These items were prized by people in the United States.

In Josefina's day, the arrival of a wagon train brought great excitement. The people of Santa Fe lined the streets, shouting *"Los americanos!"* In the plaza, banners waved in the breeze, and puppet shows or plays entertained the crowds. At night, the traders left their camps outside of town to enjoy dances and gambling in Santa Fe's inns, where fights often broke out. No proper girl or young woman went outside her home without an adult or a servant to accompany her. Josefina and Francisca were very disobedient and daring to venture out alone at night!

*This engraving shows American traders at a **fandango**, or dance party, in Santa Fe in 1825. New Mexican dances and gambling games were very popular with the American traders.*

Glossary of Spanish Words

Abuelita *(ah-bweh-LEE-tah)*—Grandma

Abuelito *(ah-bweh-LEE-toh)*—Grandpa

adiós *(ah-dee-OHS)*—good-bye

adobe *(ah-DOH-beh)*—a building material made of earth mixed with straw and water

americano *(ah-meh-ree-KAH-no)*—a man from the United States

bienvenido *(bee-en-veh-NEE-doh)*—welcome

buenos días *(BWEH-nohs DEE-ahs)*—good morning

Camino Real *(kah-MEE-no rey-AHL)*—the main road or trail that ran from Mexico City to New Mexico. Its name means "Royal Road."

fandango *(fahn-DAHN-go)*—a big celebration or party that includes lively dancing

gracias *(GRAH-see-ahs)*—thank you

los americanos *(lohs ah-meh-ree-KAH-nohs)*—the Americans

piñón *(pee-NYOHN)*—a kind of short, scrubby pine that produces delicious nuts

plaza *(PLAH-sah)*—an open square in a village or town

rancho (*RAHN-cho*)—a farm or ranch where crops are grown and animals are raised

rebozo (*reh-BO-so*)—a long shawl worn by girls and women

sala (*SAH-lah*)—a large room in a house

San Miguel (*SAHN mee-GEHL*)—Saint Michael

Santa Fe (*SAHN-tah FEH*)—the capital city of New Mexico. The words mean "Holy Faith."

señor (*seh-NYOR*)—Mr. or sir

señorita (*seh-nyo-REE-tah*)—Miss or young lady

sí (*SEE*)—yes

tía (*TEE-ah*)—aunt